GOOSE
Anna

Sandra Ann Horn was born in Wiltshire
and now lives in Southampton with
her husband and three children.
She lectures at Southampton University,
but has always loved writing.
Her first book for children was
published in 1995. *Tattybogle* was
shortlisted for both the Smarties Prize
and the Kurt Maschler Award.

A Catalogue record for this book is available from the British Library

ISBN 0340 79139X

Printed and bound in Great Britain by
Guernsey Press Ltd, Guernsey, Channel Islands

Hodder Children's Books
A Division of Hodder Headline Limited
338 Euston Road
London NW1 3BH

GOOSE Anna

Sandra Ann Horn

Illustrated by Mark Hearld

Hodder
Children's
Books

a division of Hodder Headline Limited

For my dear friend Di,
whose beautiful gift inspired this story,
with love

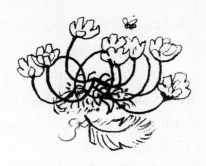

Chapter 1

It was a dark day for the people of Zaragond when Piker came amongst them. No one knew where he came from; no one saw him arrive. Early one morning, when the traders' carts pulled in to the market square, he was already there.

He might have been handsome once, the women said, but something had twisted his face into a bitter leer. He had set up a trestle table with leather

and lasts and cobbler's tools, and a sign:
Shoes made and repaired.

'Excuse me, Mister,' said Mog the
apple woman, 'but that's Hubert's pitch.
He's been selling fish there for thirty
years. It's nice and shady, see?'

'Too bad,' snarled Piker, 'it's my
pitch now – unless he wants to make
something of it.'

Hubert was old and frail, and he didn't want any trouble. He moved to another place.

People muttered about the surly stranger with no manners, but the truth was, they were pleased to see a cobbler. There wasn't one in the town, and they had half a day's trek to get their shoes and boots mended.

'Where are you from?' they asked him.

'Here and there,' said Piker.

'Are you staying?'

'I might.'

'Friendly sort of chap, isn't he?' said the townsfolk amongst themselves.

Piker was ill-tempered and he kept himself to himself, but he was a marvel with shoe-leather. He could turn his hand to making anything from great clumpy boots to dainty dancing shoes. His boots and shoes neither rubbed nor pinched,

and his repairs were neat and long-lasting.
Best of all, his prices were very cheap.

'You're just what the town needed,'
folks said to him, and he nodded, and
smiled an ugly, secretive smile to himself,
as if to say, 'if only you knew!'

By and by, they did know, but it
was too late then.

Every year, the people of Zaragond
marked the changing of the seasons by the
coming and going of great flocks of wild
geese. The meadows along the river bank
were their breeding grounds.

As soon as the last of the frosts
melted from the sedges, the townsfolk
began to gaze up at the sky
at every chance they had.
The first person to cry 'Geese
hoi!' was given a purse of
silver and a hogshead of
good ale by the mayor.

8

The leather of the purse and the oak of the barrel were the finest money could buy, and they were exhibited in the winners' houses long after the contents were spent and drunk.

The coming of the geese was always marked with joyful celebrations. They were said to bring the spring on their wings. There was feasting and dancing in the streets.

'Goose-cakes' were baked, shaped like wings and frosted white with sugar.

The children sang:

In winter's cold the field and fold
Are white with palls of snow
The winter nights are long
Ice stills the river's song

At winter's cease the welcome geese
Bring springtime on their wings
The days grow warm and long
Sweet is the river's song

Anna had grown up singing that
song, in the big house on the harbour.
Her father Gianto was a merchant, with
a fleet of fine ships. He had married late
in life, and when his young wife died
giving birth to their only child, he buried
his grief in his work and his collection
of old, rare books.

Meantime, his child was growing
up pretty, wilful, and doted on by
everyone in the house. Everyone who
knew her called her 'a proper little
princess' when she got her own way
by sweetness and smiles, and 'a proper
little madam' when she frowned and
stamped her foot.

She would have been quite spoiled
but for the wise and loving care of Cara,
her mother's old nurse. It was Cara who
bathed Anna's grazed knees, wiped
away her tears, sang her to sleep at
night and woke her with a morning kiss.

It was also Cara who said when it was time for bed and meant it, and insisted that cabbage must be eaten up or there would be no pudding.

The demands of the business meant that Gianto was often away from home, but when he returned his time and care were all for Anna. Her world was sheltered from all harm.

Chapter 2

Soon after he arrived, there was a rumour that Piker was living in an old tumble-down cottage on the edge of the town. When one of the bolder market women asked him outright, he smiled his thin twisted smile and said, 'That's for me to know.'

The cottage had been empty for who-knows-how-long. All the windows were broken and the roof had fallen in. No one could remember who it had once belonged to. It had always been known as The Ruin.

When the word went round that Piker had moved into it, some of the men from the town and a couple of lads walked out to visit him one Sunday afternoon, with tools and paint, to help him out a bit. They took slashers and billhooks with them too, because the path to the cottage was overgrown by thick coils of brambles.

When they got close to where the path turned off the main track, they were baffled.

'This isn't the right way! We've come wrong somewhere.'

'We should have turned off further back.'

'No! I'll swear this is it. I've been here blackberrying hundreds of times before now – the path runs to the left of that old gnarly oak.'

'Well where is it then?'
There was no path.
There were no
brambles. A little way
in past the trees was a
tall hedge of thorn bushes,
close planted and several
feet thick.
'How did that get there?'
'He must have planted 'em.'
'Never! Look at the height
of them. They've been
here years.'

'They have not, then! I told
you, I come blackberrying here. I picked
the last lot not a month ago, and my
missus has got the pots of jam to prove it!'

They scratched their heads and
argued for a while, then walked along the
hedge to look for a gate. There wasn't a
gap anywhere.

'Here, young Tom, shin up that tree
and see if you can see anything.'

Young Tom went up the tree like a
squirrel. He climbed until he could see
clear over the thorn hedge, then shinned
along an overhanging branch.

'Can you see anything?' the others
called up to him. Then he seemed to
freeze, his eyes fixed on something the
others could not see.

17

'Tom! What's up?' they called.

He did not answer. Then he shook his head as if coming out of a dream.

He pointed over the hedge.

'It's ...' and that was the last word anyone ever heard him speak. He was struck dumb.

'He's been taken in some kind of fit,' they said, and they piggy-backed him home and sent for the doctor.

The doctor recommended warm poultices to his throat and honey linctus. It was no good. He tried balsam inhalations, hot brandy and hypnotism. They did not work either. The doctor shook his head.

Tom never spoke again. His mother gave him a slate and pencil, so he could write what he could no longer say, but his hand shook so badly that no one ever made out what it was meant to be.

'Lost his wits, poor soul,' they said.

Next market day, the talk was all of poor young Tom and the strange fit he'd had up in the tree.

'Terrible thing, isn't it?' Mog the apple woman said to Piker. He smiled. 'One less wagging tongue,' he said.

The apple woman was shocked. 'You nasty creature! What a vile thing to say!' she shouted at him. 'I'll go barefoot before I buy shoes from you again, you cold-hearted viper!' Piker looked at her with hate in his eyes, then he slipped a smooth dark stone out of his pocket and thrust it towards her.

Mog stared at the stone as if she could not look away. In its black depths was a fiery red eye, and it drew Mog's gaze. At last, Piker closed his fingers over it. Mog shook her head as if she was dazed, then turned away. She went back to her stall and began to cry out, 'Apples! Fresh juicy fruit!' but instead of stopping to buy, folk hurried past with looks of disgust on their faces.

Mog's hands were covered in oozing, bleeding boils, so crowded together there was scarcely room for a pin between them. At first she was puzzled. Then she looked down and saw her hands, and began to scream. The doctor bathed Mog's putrid skin with tincture of elacampane.

'I've never even had a pimple in my life!' she howled, 'why should this happen now, and so badly too?'

'I have no idea,' said the doctor,
'it's probably something you ate or
touched, but this will clear it up.
Drink only spring water for three days
and eat plenty of green vegetables
and fruit.'

'Fruit!' said Mog, 'there's more
than enough of that! Nobody will buy
my apples for fear they'll catch what
I've got!'

'Patience, woman,' said the doctor.
But patience didn't help, and nor did
the tincture. Mog's skin remained in its
horrible state. She stayed indoors, for
fear of the disgust in people's eyes
whenever they saw her, and never sold
another apple.

The more she thought about it – and
she had plenty of time for thinking –
the more she believed that Piker was
responsible in some way, but she was

afraid to say so to anyone. She did not
know how far his powers reached, and
she did not want to bring more trouble
upon herself.

Chapter 3

For a while, the townspeople did not suspect Piker. They thought that Tom and Mog were simply unlucky to be stricken with illness. Then the 'bad luck' began to spread – a crop of ugly warts here, a withered arm there – and always it happened to someone who had upset Piker, although not one of them could give an account of the dark stone afterwards.

People began to be uneasy, but they did not discuss their suspicions openly, because they too were afraid. And after all, they said, warts or the palsy can happen to anyone ...

It was not until Cara took Anna to fetch her new dancing shoes that they knew, beyond the shadow of a doubt, the evil that was in their midst.

'Hurry, hurry!' called Anna on the morning they were to fetch the new shoes. She had chosen the soft, rose-red leather and silver buckles herself from Piker's finest stock. Her father had been away from home on a trading voyage, and he was due home at any moment.

Anna was determined to be wearing her rose-red shoes when she showed him the new dance she had been learning. She hopped up and down with impatience while Cara

struggled to fasten her cloak. She ran and
skipped all the way to the market square,
with Cara panting along behind her.

Piker saw them coming, and put the shoes on the table ready.

'We've come for my shoes, please, Mr Piker,' said Anna.

'There they are before you, little Miss,' he leered.

Anna's pretty face grew dark.

'Those are not my shoes!' she cried, 'they're the wrong colour! I chose rose-red, not red-red.'

'You are mistaken, Miss,' snarled Piker. Anna shook her head.

'I am not, and I won't have them!'

Piker's brow darkened. He reached under his cloak and drew out the dark stone, just as Cara came panting up to the stall. Anna burst into tears and flung her face in Cara's apron.

It was Cara who found herself gazing into the depths of the stone and unable to look away. Then Piker put the stone away, and she blinked.

'Temper, temper, Mr Piker!' said Cara. She bent to soothe Anna and dry her eyes. 'There, my little love! Don't cry any more – ooh! How my poor ears do pain me all of a sudden!'

'Poor Cara! Let me see,' said Anna.

'No, my dove, we'll get along home and I'll see to it then,' said Cara. She turned to Piker, 'As for you, Sir, you'll be hearing from my master about your behaviour.'

'I look forward to that, I'm sure,' he replied, with honey in his voice and poison in his eyes.

Cara and Anna hurried home. Inside the house, Cara snatched off her hat, which felt too tight all of a sudden, and looked in the mirror this way and that,

to see why her ears felt so strange. She
gasped. Her ears were thick and pink
and hairy and pointed. Pig's ears.

Cara sat down heavily. 'Whatever–?
Am I dreaming?' she said.

Anna, white with shock, screamed
out, 'Piker! Piker did that! Fetch my
Daddy, someone, quickly!'

Anna's father came at a run in response to the garbled message from a hysterical kitchenmaid. Cara could give no clear account of the events, so stunned was she, but Anna was certain that Piker was responsible. 'He showed a stone to Cara – it's bad magic. Send him away, Daddy! And get someone to make Cara better!'

Gianto listened carefully to his daughter's account of the morning. He asked questions, particularly about the stone.

'I will certainly see Mr Piker off and out of our town, and I will see what can be done for Cara,' he promised. He called for the doctor, who simply shook his head. It was beyond his skill to help.

Anna's father ordered soft silk bonnets to be stitched by the sewing-room maids, to cover the ugliness of Cara's ears.

Then he shut himself up with his
books and sent word that he was not to
be disturbed, even by Anna.

During his travels, Anna's father
had collected a great library of old
and rare books from all over the world.

Many of them concerned the magical arts. It was to these books he turned for any information he could discover.

Eventually, after days and days of searching and reading, he found, in the oldest, dustiest volume of all, a reference to dark stones:

> *There are known to be seven dark stones of great power. They were quarried in an age long past, from a deep seam in Old Myringia. They are fire obsidian. In their black depths lies an eye of glowing red, in which their power resides.*
>
> *The outer parts are smooth and black, and shaped like a coiled snake. It is said that the stones themselves choose who may use their power and who may not.*

In the hands of a chosen one,
they are capable of transforming
human flesh and human form.
Those who look upon them are
compelled to gaze at the eye, and
it is at that time the curse may
be made.

The curses are
life-long unless
love's kiss
breaks them.

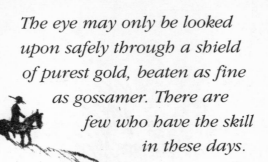

*The eye may only be looked
upon safely through a shield
of purest gold, beaten as fine
as gossamer. There are
few who have the skill
in these days.*

Anna's father
marked the
place in the
book with great
care. He thought, long
and carefully, about what he
should do.

Then he sent for the
keys to his treasure-
house, and the
finest
goldsmiths
in the land.

ZARAGOND

Chapter 4

His success in cursing Tom and Mog and the others had given Piker great confidence. The power had gone to his head and made him careless of his own safety. The boils and other blights he had inflicted on people could be explained away as natural events, but now he had made pig's ears grow on Cara's head – and Anna had seen the stone. The secret of his evil magic was out.

'So be it,' said Piker, 'it is time they knew their Master.'

He had not reckoned with Gianto.

In a light and airy room at the top of the big house, the pick of all the goldsmiths in the land had begun their work on sheets of thrice-refined purest gold.

Their task was to beat the gold into sheets as fine as gossamer, without even the smallest hole or tear. Their hammers were padded with softest doeskin, with sable, with silk velvet. They wore powerful eye-glasses. One by one they left, as the gold was as thin as they could make it and yet not thin enough for Gianto.

Meantime, Anna stitched silken linings for Cara's bonnets; she would let no one else do the work. Every morning and every evening, she bathed the poor ears with warm water and her own tears,

and smoothed ointments on to the
tough skin. She could not be persuaded
otherwise by Cara, or her father, or
anyone else. Were the poor ears too
warm? She sprinkled them with the
finest cologne. Were they too cold?
She warmed them in her hands.

On the night before the disaster,
she smothered them in loving,
remorseful kisses, and so broke Piker's
curse, but she was never to know it.

The next morning, long before the
household was awake, Anna's father
went to the room at the top of the house
and inspected the goldsmiths' work.

All over the tables were sheets of
gold beaten so fine that the draft from
the door lifted them into the air. He
picked up each one and held it in front
of his eyes. Then he shook his head and
put it down.

It was not until he picked up the seventh sheet that he found what he was looking for. Gold so fine he could see through it, like gauze, evenly beaten and with not a blemish on it anywhere. It was on the table of Anselm, the oldest goldsmith of them all; a man so frail and bent that Gianto had almost sent him away at the beginning, believing that he could not possibly do the work.

'Let me try,' Anselm had said,
'My strength is not in my muscles but
in my mind: it is patience. It is a gift
of my old age.' He beat the gold sheet
down gently, slowly, little by little,
until he had made a perfect sheet of
gossamer-thin metal.

Gianto laid the gold carefully
across a circle of glass, set in a frame
like a hand mirror. When he held it
up in front of his face, he could see
everything through a faint golden haze.

'That will do,' he said.

He roused his trusted servants, and
sent them secretly through the town to
warn everyone to stay indoors until they
were given the all-clear. He sent for a
good sharp pitchfork from the
stable. Then, he set out for the
market square, with the
golden glass hidden
under his cloak.

His plan was to confront Piker, and drive him out of the town. If he could get his hands on the stone and destroy it, so much the better. He had thought it out with great care, and it would have worked perfectly – but for Anna.

The early morning bustle in the house had roused her from her bed, and her first thought was for her father. She ran through the house looking for him. The servants had been told to keep her indoors at all costs, and not to tell her what her father was doing.

When she could not find him, and no one would tell her where he was, she guessed that he was out after Piker. She could not bear it that he was facing danger alone, when she had been the cause of it.

When the servants were distracted about
the breakfast, she put on an old shabby
cloak and slipped out unnoticed through
the back door.

Anna's father strode through the frosty air of the autumn morning, towards the square. Piker had already set up his stall, and was looking around with a puzzled frown on his face at the empty market place.

He was uneasy. He knew the townsfolk were mortally afraid of him, and he did not think them capable of standing up for themselves, but where were they?

Chapter 5

His sense of power over them had been growing daily, and he was ready to take over the town. He had not reckoned with Gianto the merchant, whom he had never met.

'Piker!' The loud, angry shout from Anna's father chilled his blood for a moment. Then he grinned to himself and slipped the stone out of his pocket. He swung round, holding it out towards his challenger.

Anna's father lifted the golden mask
up over his eyes. Then he thrust
the points of the pitchfork at Piker.

'Out! Out you go, you devil's
whelp!'

Jab!

'That's for Tom!'

Jab!

'That's for Mog!'

Jab! Jab!

'That's for Cara!'

Piker was backing off, moving
faster with every lunge of the pitchfork.
Anna's father drove him relentlessly
towards the bridge over the river. As
he did so, he slid his hand down the
handle of the fork, trying to shorten
the distance between himself and
Piker, so that he could snatch the stone.

'No you don't!' snarled Piker.
Afraid and cornered though he was,
he was not going to give up so easily.

He put the hand with the stone behind his back. At the same time, he unfastened his cloak with the other hand and hurled it at Anna's father. The cloak wrapped itself round his head, and he stumbled, momentarily blinded. Piker took his chance, turned and ran.

At the town gate on the bridge, he turned and held the dark stone high above his head. He gazed around with hate in his eyes, looking for one last chance to show his power and to hurt the people who had cast him out. The streets were still deserted.

Then Anna ran round the corner, crying out for her father. Piker called her name, and she looked up at the stone. The world seemed first to stand still and then to vanish as she gazed into the blazing red eye. Then the pain began.

45

Anna's screams rang in her father's ears like a death-knell. He snatched the cloak from round his head and hurled it to the ground. He gazed frantically around. Where was she? What was happening to her?

The screaming stopped and a low mournful cry hung in the air. He looked back towards the corner, and then he knew. His poor old heart skipped a beat at what he saw, then a great black tide of grief surged through him and his heart stopped for ever.

He stumbled forwards, and with his dying strength he launched the pitchfork at Piker's head. The pitchfork missed its mark, but caught Piker on the wrist. His arm jerked upwards. The dark stone flew out of his hand and plunged down into the river. It fell deep into the black, thick mud on the riverbed, and for ought I know it lies there still.

Piker shrieked in torment as it fell, and then ran for his life, over the bridge and away. He ran through the goosefields, and the birds flew up all round him, calling out in alarm.

Their cries and the beating of their great white wings filled the air as they soared up over the town.

The townsfolk came running out of their houses, and clustered round the lifeless body of Anna's father. Many of them wept as they picked him up and carried him into the big house on the quay.

The doctor tried long and in vain to revive the brave old man. It was only later, when they all knew there was no hope, that someone said, 'But where's Anna?'

'She saw her father fall,' said one, 'I expect the poor little mite has hidden herself somewhere in fright and sorrow. We must find her.' They searched the house from roof to cellar, and the garden. Then they spread out over the quay and the ships, and all through the town.

They searched the empty goose fields, grass blade by grass blade. Anna was nowhere to be found.

Late that night, they all went home to bed and vowed to search again the next day. They never found her.

When the hubbub had died down, the geese settled once again on their nests, but not for long. They were restless. The frosty autumn air and the shortening days told them it was time to prepare for the long flight to their winter home.

The next morning, the first skein of geese took to the air. They flew like a great curved spear-head, calling until their cries were lost in the vast blue distances of the sky.

Day by day, the flocks of geese left the fields along the river and flew away. The older birds led the way, soaring high on slow, strong wing-beats.

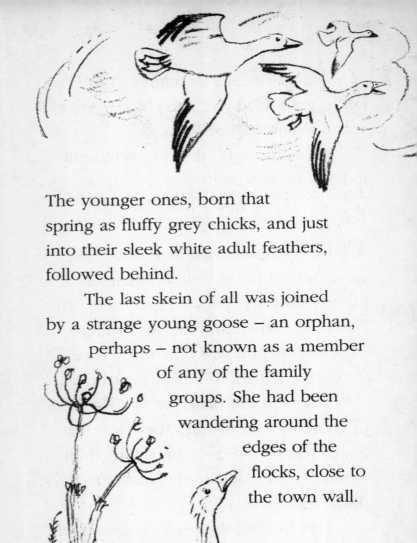

The younger ones, born that
spring as fluffy grey chicks, and just
into their sleek white adult feathers,
followed behind.

The last skein of all was joined
by a strange young goose – an orphan,
perhaps – not known as a member
of any of the family
groups. She had been
wandering around the
edges of the
flocks, close to
the town wall.

She had watched as skein after skein left, but it was not until the last that she joined in.

All the others had taken to the sky before she too allowed her great white wings to lift her up and away from Zaragond. She joined the end of the skein as the geese called their farewells, but she herself was silent. Below on the river bank, nothing remained but a drift of white down from the empty nests.

Chapter 5

Thousands and thousands of miles from Zaragond, over the mountains and over the sea, was the great salt-marsh of Rotherholme. It lay under the foothills of a great range of stony peaks which gave it shelter from the north.

Winter brought its share of frost and snow to the marsh, but the cold did not strike too deep nor last too long. Even in the darkest months of the year, grasses and sedges grew along the banks.

When the first frosts spiced the
air, the long curving skeins of wild
geese flew over a low stone cottage
on the edge of the salt-marsh. They
came every year with the October
moon; the marsh was their winter
feeding ground. All through the day
and on into evening, the sky was filled
with the beating of their wings and their
mournful cries.

Old Meg and her son Jack watched
the geese as they circled in the sky,
then flew down amongst the marsh
grasses and began building their nests.
Soon, the marsh was carpeted in white
feathery mounds as far as Meg and
Jack could see.

'Looks like it's been snowing,'
said Jack.

'Aye, and soon enough, it will be,'
said his mother, 'we must get the logs in.'

Meg and
Jack lived in the
stone cottage. They
earned their living baking
bread. Every morning, long
before the sun was up, Jack
stoked the fire and Meg set
the yeast to warm.

By breakfast-time, the smell
of new-baked bread filled the air,
and folk in the nearby village
breathed in deeply,
mmmmm!

They knew
that Jack
would soon be
arriving with a basket of golden crisp-
crusted loaves. Bread from Meg's cottage
was the best in the land; good enough
to put a smile on the face of the
town clock, folk said.

Jack was reckoned to be a
bit simple by the village folk.

He smiled and nodded when he
brought the bread, but he rarely spoke.
The truth is, he was very shy – and
at home, Meg did the talking for both
of them.

In the evenings, when the work
was done, they
sat by the fire in
contentment.

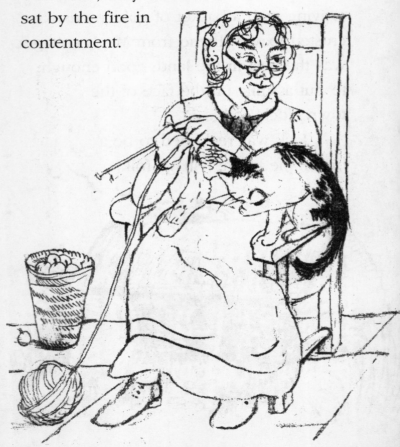

Jack carved the wooden paddles and kneading boards for the bread, and Meg knitted socks and told the old stories to while away the time.

The pattern of their lives stayed much the same year upon year, and

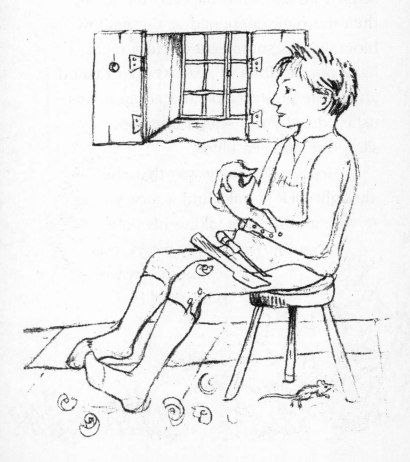

it suited them well. They loved to watch the light change the pools from silver to rose and gold as the sun set each day.

They kept account of the changing seasons by watching the colours in the marsh; first the white and pale pink of scurvybite and thrift dappled the grass, then the pink deepened as the mallow bloomed. As summer drew to a close, hazy purple drifts of sea-lavender floated above the grass stalks, and autumn was ushered in by the scarlet tinges on samphire and sea-blite.

Meg's only worry was that she thought Jack should find a nice young wife and he was taking his time about it. Jack's only worry was that his mother was becoming frail.

Her hands were often knotted and
painful in the colder weather. Neither
of them spoke of their fears to the other.

Meg's and Jack's lives might have gone
on in the same old way for ever, but the
world was changing round them. Far
away, a war was being fought on land
and on sea. They knew nothing of it
until its ugliness reached out across the
land, to the village and the salt-marsh.

One bright frosty morning, Jack
was out with the bread when he met
three strangers. One held out his hand
and said, 'Good day to you, my fine
fellow!' Jack smiled and shook the
stranger's hand. As he did, he felt
something cold in his palm. It was a
silver coin. The stranger said, 'Right my
lad! You have taken the King's shilling
and must come with me. His Majesty
needs strong men to sail his ships.'

Jack turned to run, but the men
grabbed him and marched him away,
while the new loaves tumbled into
the mud.

Old Meg waited and waited for her
son to come home. When it was long
past his usual time, she hobbled out
across the marsh towards the village,
to find out what had happened.

Half way along the path, she found
the basket and the bread all over the
ground. Her heart thumped wildly in
her chest and she cried out, 'Jack! Oh,
Jack!' She looked round and about, and
called his name over and over. The
marsh was silent. Too shocked to walk
on, she staggered to a grassy hummock
and sat down to catch her breath.

She was still sitting there in a daze
when some of the village women came
along, to see where their bread had got
to. Before they reached her, Meg could

hear them chattering about the Press
Gang coming, and how their menfolk
had got wind of it, and hid.

'Bad luck to them, evil varmin!'
said one woman, 'at least they didn't
get none of our men.'

Then Meg knew.

Chapter 6

Far from his home on the salt-marsh and all its joys and comforts, Jack found life at sea hard to endure. He had always been shy, and was not able to join in the rough banter with the rest of the crew. He made no friends, although he was respected as a good steady worker.

At night, on watch or sleepless in his rolling hammock, he thought about Meg and wondered how she was

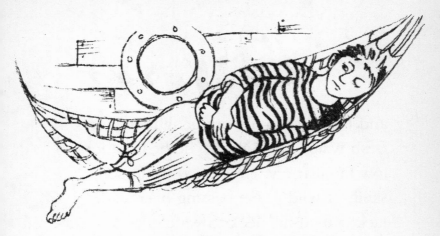

managing without him. He thought
about how her hands stiffened and
swelled in the cold weather, and he'd
had to help her knead the dough. He
knew she could not carry the full basket
of bread round the village.

He was anxious for her, but all the
time the ship bore him further and
further away and there was nothing he
could do to ease his heartache but to
keep busy.

One morning, the ship was at
anchor in the bay of a small island,

and Jack was in a work-gang taking on fresh water. High above, he heard a long low familiar cry. He looked up to see a skein of wild geese passing overhead. Jack craned his neck to watch them.

'I wonder if they're our geese,' he said to himself, 'perhaps they are going to their nests round the cottage. If only I could give them a message for my mother!'

'Stop day-dreaming and get a move on with that bucket!' cut across his thoughts, and with a weary sigh he turned his mind back to his work.

The strange young goose was weary and frightened. The skein had been flying for many long hours without resting, over the mountains and across a seemingly endless ocean. She had no idea where they were going, or what her fate would be. Every beat of her wings took her further from her home. The skein flew on through a sunset which tinged their wings with flame, into a deepening twilight. She began to think she would spend all the rest of her life on the wing, until she could fly no longer, and would plunge down into the deep cold waters below.

Then at last the leader gave a long low call and began to fly downwards. He headed for a cluster of small islands, and the skein followed. They landed on the green turf close to the shoreline, to graze and to rest as night fell.

The young goose stayed on the fringes of the flock and grazed alone.

By and by, goose families clustered together, snuggled their heads under their white wings and slept.

The young goose slept apart and alone. In the morning, she woke to the sound of human voices close by. There was something in the sound that was comforting and familiar. She waddled in the direction it came from, to a fresh water stream where the sailors were filling their kegs.

'Hello!' said Jack, 'what are you doing here then, my pretty?' He reached out and smoothed the young goose gently. 'Perhaps,' he said, 'you really are going to our salt-marsh. Mayhap you'll see my mother.' He broke up some biscuit, moistened it with water, and fed her. He scooped water into his hands so that she could drink. The young goose could not thank him for his kindness, she could only hiss or

squawk, so she kept her peace, but she
stayed close by.

The geese rested for a few more
hours, the skein on the grassy
banks of the island and the
young one in the
warmth of Jack's
arms. Then the
leader gave a
loud call and
took to the sky,
with the others
close behind.

Jack stood up. 'You must go with them,' he said, 'this isn't the place for you. If perchance you see my mother, give her this from me.' He dropped a soft sweet kiss on her feathered head and cast her into the air.

Chapter 7

Without Jack, there began a time of sorrow and heavy work for Meg. She grieved sorely for her dear son.

When the wild geese came back to the marsh on the wings of winter, her hands were very painful and swollen. She could not knead the dough well, and folk complained that the bread was lumpy. She could not manage to deliver the loaves either, without Jack. Only a few kind folk came to the cottage for

a penny loaf and said they didn't mind
the lumpy bits.

Every evening, Meg sat by the fire
alone, her knitting idle in her hands.
Every night, she set a lamp in the
window in the vain hope that Jack
might come home, to light
his way across
the marsh.

With the warmer weather, the
geese left the marsh and flew south.
Drifts of white feathers blew among the
spring flowers. Meg's hands grew strong
again in the sun, and she managed the
work better. She did not cease to grieve
for Jack, but her spirit was lighter
through the summer days.

As the year rolled round and
the mists of autumn veiled the marsh,
she began to be afraid. Every day,
she watched the sky and listened.
She was looking for the skeins of
wild geese, and listening for their
cries. 'I have always loved to watch
the geese return,' said Meg, 'but now
I dread it. With them will come the
cold cruel winter, and my aches and
pains. What will become of me when
I can't make the bread properly?'

The very next morning, as the
sun came up, Meg heard the first of
the wild geese calling across the sky.
She sat in the chimney corner and
wept. The fire stayed unlit. When
customers tapped on the door, she did
not answer.

That night, Meg lit the lamp and
set it in the window, as she had done
every night since Jack was taken away.

Suddenly, she heard the whirring of great wings close by. She ran to open the door.

A young girl was standing on the step. A girl with a sweet face and a dainty body, but stumpy legs and wide flat feet. A single white feather was plaited into her hair.

'Please may I come in out of the dark?' she said, 'I am far from home and lost.'

'Come in and be welcome,' said Meg.

'I have not much, but what there is, we will share, for the sake of my own dear one, who is also far from his home. What is your name?' The young girl's eyes filled with tears.

'I can't remember,' she said.

'Come and sit by the fire. Rest, and eat,' said Meg. 'Perhaps it will come back to you in a while. Meantime, I'll just call you dearie.'

Later, Meg sat by the girl as she slept and softly, slowly spoke all the names she could think of. 'Abigail, Adelaide, Agnes, Alice, Amina, Anna,' she began. When she reached Anna, the girl stirred in her sleep and smiled.

'That will do,' said Meg.

In the morning, she said, 'Would you like oatmeal for your breakfast, Anna?' and the girl said, 'Yes, please.' Anna stayed with Meg through the winter, helping her with making the

bread and delivering it round the village.
They shared the simple food and the
work of the house. Day by day Anna
waddled over the marsh on her stubby
legs, carrying the basket of loaves. The
village boys mocked her.

They walked behind, imitating her
waddling walk, and they called her
'Goose-Anna.' Sometimes she cried, but
she did not let Meg see the tears.

In the evenings, Anna stitched a coverlet
with a design of red roofed houses along
a river on which sailed
proud ships.

'That's pretty, my
dear,' said Meg, 'where
did you learn that
pattern?'

'I don't know,'
said Anna.

Once, in the warm
glow of the fire, she began
to sing: 'At winter's cease the
welcome ...' She stopped.

'Go on,' said Meg, 'that's a sweet tune.'

Anna shook her head. 'I can't
remember any more.'

75

As the pleasant evenings went on,
Meg took up her knitting once more
and told many tales of her dear Jack.
The talking eased her heart a little.
She grew to love Anna like a daughter.

When the first pale spring flowers
opened on the marsh and the days
grew warm, Meg's hands were stronger
once more. Anna was restless
and uneasy.

She sat, tense in her chair in the evenings and could not settle to her needlework.

'What's the matter?' said Meg, but Anna did not know. She slept fitfully, and dreamed night after night of a great red eye, pulling her away from the safety of Meg's cottage and into the unknown.

The first skeins of geese took to the skies. Anna watched them. She grew sadder as the days went by. One morning, a tear dropped on Meg's face as she slept, and a voice whispered, 'Goodbye, Mother Meg. I will try to come again.' Meg stirred and thought that she was dreaming, but when she rose from her bed Anna was not in the house. Meg ran to the door.

Anna was out on the marsh amongst the last of the geese.

The next moment the air was full of
beating wings. Anna and the geese had
gone. Meg cried out, and the wild geese
echoed the sound as they flew.

Chapter 7

Meg worked alone through the summer. Every morning she gazed around the marsh as if expecting to see her dear ones hurrying across it, but they did not come. Every evening, she thought long and lovingly about her lost Jack and lost Anna. Every night, she set the lamp, in case one or other of them came home in the dark.

Soon after the first frost silvered the grass and the leaves, Meg heard the

beating of great wings one night. She
ran to open the door. Anna was
standing on the step. 'Here I am, Mother
Meg,' she said. Meg opened her arms
and gathered the dear girl in.

'Where have you been all these
long months, my dear?' she asked, after
supper. Anna shook her head. 'I don't
know. I can't remember.'

'What do you do when you're
away?' asked Meg. Anna frowned. 'I
don't know. I have forgotten.'

The years went by, as years do. For
two more winters, when the wild geese
returned, Anna came with them. For
three more springs, when the geese left,
Anna left too. In that time, she grew to
be a beautiful young woman, but her
stubby legs and flat feet stayed as
stubby and flat as ever.

On many evenings as they sat
together after the work was done, Meg
wanted to ask Anna questions, but she
could not find the words.

Then one evening when she knew
the time was short and Anna would

soon be gone with the geese,
she found the courage. She
said, 'My dear, I know you
are under some kind of spell.
Won't you tell me about it?
Perhaps I can think of a
way to help.'

Anna jumped up in fright.
'Hush, Mother Meg! It is
forbidden to speak of it! Please
never mention it again, if you love
me.' She ran out of the room. Meg
did not speak of it again, but she
thought all the more.

The third winter was
halfway past when one morning Anna
called out, 'Someone's coming.' Meg came
to the door and shaded her eyes.

'He has the look of my dear Jack,' she
said, 'except that
he walks as
if the ground
was rolling
under
his feet.'

The stranger drew nearer.

'He DOES look like my Jack,'
said Meg, 'except for the pigtail in his
hair.' The stranger began to run and
call, 'Ma! I'm home!'

Well, they were up half the night,
talking and laughing, hugging and
weeping. Anna sat quietly in the corner
while Meg told Jack how she had come
like a blessing out of the sky. 'But you
won't need me now,' she said, 'so I'll
be on my way in the morning.' They
would not hear of it, of course. She
must stay. Jack would sleep in the
hayloft and be glad to. So that's how
it was.

As the days and weeks went by, Meg
saw how the two young people were
drawn to each other.

Every evening, before he went to
his bed in the hay-loft, Jack smoothed

his mother's hair and dropped a
gentle kiss on her head. Something
stirred in Anna's heart as she watched.

Jack's time at sea had been
hard and cruel, and sometimes he
fell into black moods, but gentle
Anna could always coax him out of
them. In the evenings, Jack carved a
piece of wood with his knife, but he
slipped it into his pocket if he saw
anyone watching.

One night, he wasn't quite quick
enough, and Meg saw that it was a
lovespoon. 'Wonderful! Now surely
he means to give that to Anna,' she
said to herself, but as time went on
shy Jack kept his thoughts and the
spoon to himself.

'I'll have to say something,' said
Meg under her breath.

In the morning, when she handed
him the basket of loaves, she took

a deep breath, and said, 'Our sweet
Anna will make some lucky man a
good wife.'

'To be sure,' said Jack, rather pink
in the face.

'Well–' began his mother, but Jack had bolted and was already half way to the gate. 'Botheration!' said Meg. Then she scrubbed and scrubbed the bread pans until they shone.

Spring came to Rotherholme. The breeze across the marsh blew soft and warm. Meg began to worry. 'Soon, Anna will go away again with the wild geese and I'm sure it will break Jack's heart,' she thought. 'I must think of a way to keep her here.'

She wracked her brain, but could not think until evening, when the lamplight gleamed on the white feather Anna always wore in her hair. 'There is something about that feather,' thought Meg. 'I believe it has to do with the spell on Anna. If I could take it from her it might break the spell.' She began to think how it might be done.

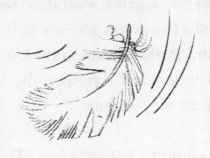

Chapter 9

Late that night, when everyone was in bed, Meg got up and crept into Anna's room. She bent over the sleeping girl and began to unwind the feather from her hair, very gently.

As she unwound one strand, Anna gave a low cry in her sleep, like the call of a wild bird. Meg stopped and drew back for a moment, in alarm, but she thought of Jack and Anna's happiness, and started to

unwind the second strand. The colour
drained from Anna's face until she was
as white as goosedown. Meg's hands
began to tremble, but she knew she
must go on. She reached for the third
and last strand of hair.

Suddenly a noise of great wings
beating filled the room, as
loud as thunder.
Meg cried out and
put her hands
over her ears.
Her cries
brought Jack
stumbling from
his bed in the loft
and running up the stairs.

'Mother, mother, where are you?
What's wrong?'

He burst into the room. He saw
Anna, pale as death, and caught her up
in his arms.

'Oh my dearest love!' He kissed
her. The white feather fell to the floor.
The noise of wings stopped. Anna
opened her eyes. She smiled
at Jack and kissed
him back. She
jumped out of bed
and danced round the
room on long slim legs
and dainty feet.

'Dearest Jack, your kiss has
broken the spell!' she laughed. 'I was
doomed to fly with the wild geese for
half the year, and to have goose legs
and feet the rest of the time, until love's
kiss freed me.' She stopped and
held out her
hands to him, 'And
you love me in spite
of my strange shape.'

'What strange shape?'
said puzzled Jack.

91

Anna danced back into his arms. Then they held out their arms for Meg too, and amidst tears and laughter Anna told them her story. She shuddered as she told them how Piker had cursed her as her father drove him away for his wickedness.

'Piker held the stone out in front of me. I did not want to look at it, but I could not help myself. It was like a great fiery eye staring at me.

'All at once, I felt myself shrinking. Something pushed and pressed inside me, and wings grew out of my back. There was a sharp pain in my face, as my nose became a hard red beak. I remember screaming in horror as my legs shrank and hardened. Scales formed on my feet; webs stretched between my toes. Feathers pierced my skin like a million pin-pricks.

'As I screamed out, I saw my father fall. He died saving me and all our town from Piker and the evil stone.'

Jack held her in his arms while she wept for her father, and when she had finished weeping she slept on his breast for a while, as she had done years before on the island in the sea.

Then he had sent her on her way with a kiss. This time, he woke her with one.

The stars were beginning to fade in the early morning sky before they all got to bed, after the talking and weeping, the laughing and making plans.

When they woke, Jack, Meg and
Anna cooked and baked and made the
house ready for the wedding feast.

Jack made fragrant spiced loaves,
plaited like golden wreaths. Anna
cleaned the windows and brought
armfuls of flowers from the marsh. Meg
dusted and swept the floor. As she did,
she caught up the white feather on the
end of her broom and tossed it outside.
It crumbled to dust and blew away on
the morning air, as the song of the wild
geese rang out for joy all around.

THE STORMTELLER

Sandra Ann Horn
Illustrated by Amanda Harvey

Zeke loved the sea. He loved listening to the music of the waves and looking for driftwood, shells and pebbles on the beach.

As soon as he was old enough, he went to sea as a cabin boy and travelled the world ...

... where he discovered something very rare and very special - a stormteller.